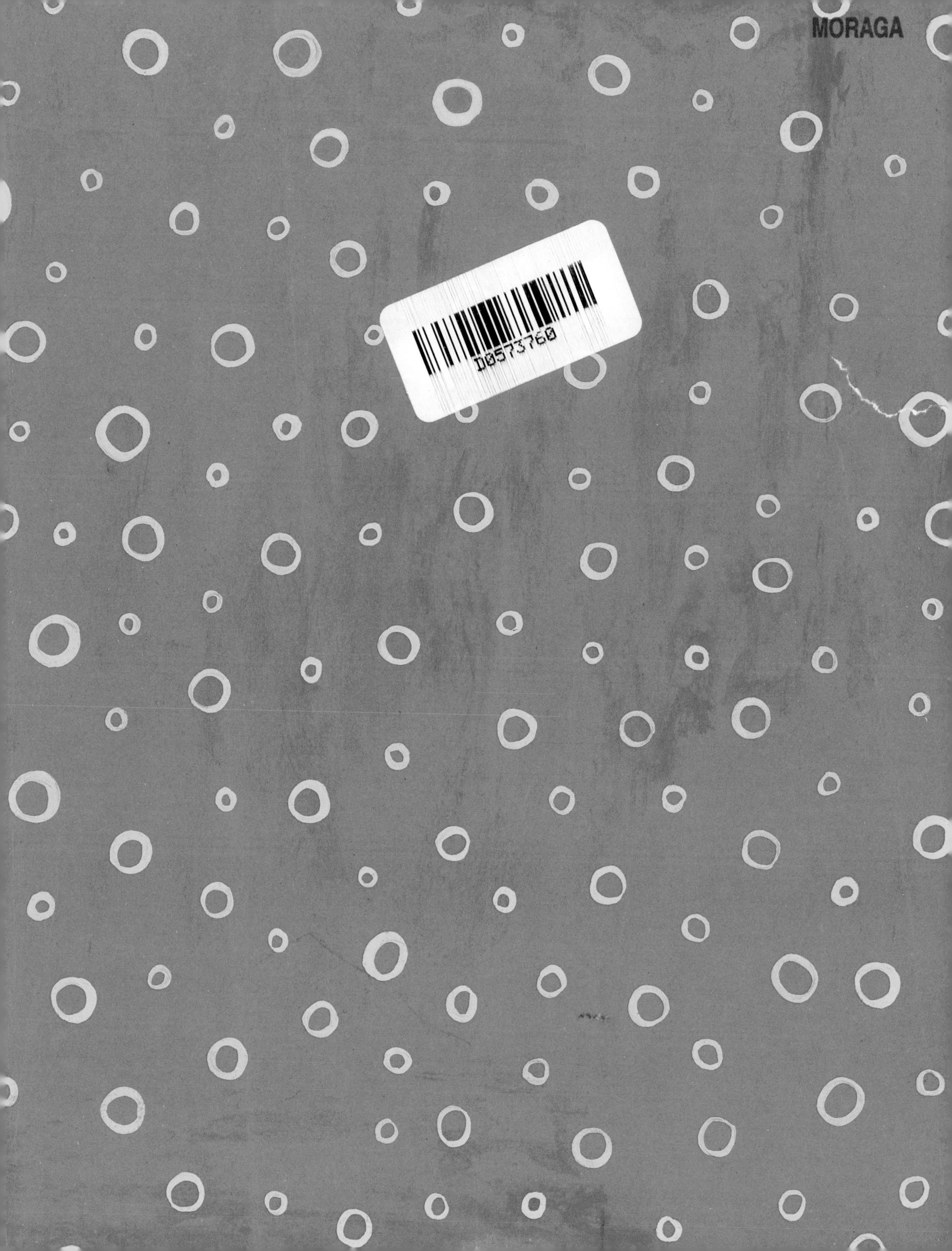
MORAGA

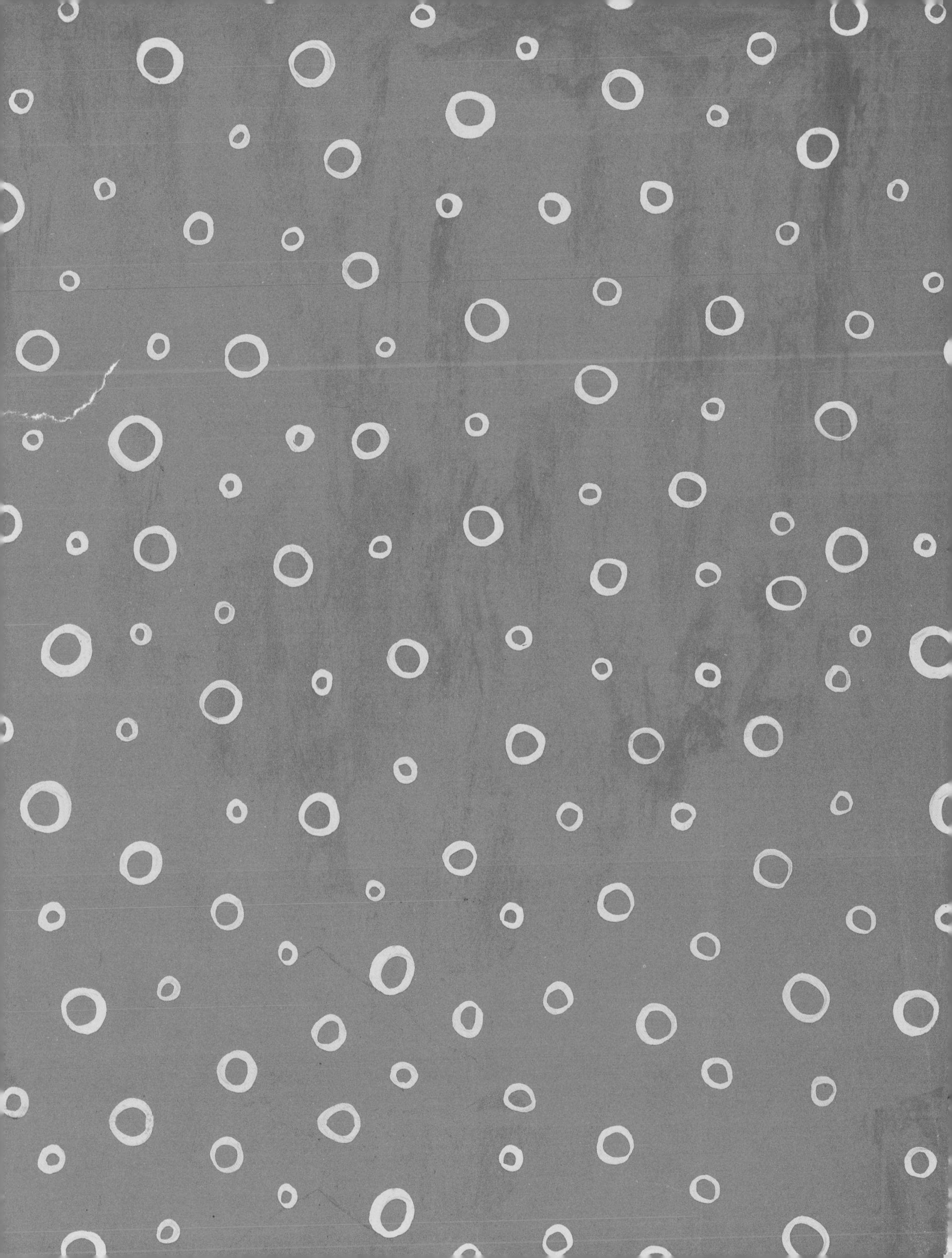

Elinor and Violet

Two Naughty Chickens at the Beach

by Patti Beling Murphy

LITTLE, BROWN AND COMPANY

New York · An AOL Time Warner Company

For my sweet girls

First Edition

Library of Congress Cataloging-in-Publication Data

Murphy, Patti Beling.
Elinor and Violet: two naughty chickens at the beach / by Patti Beling Murphy.
p. cm.
Summary: While Violet, a really naughty chicken, is visiting her grandmother again for the summer, she convinces Elinor to do things that upset Elinor's mother and sisters, but Elinor does prove to have a mind of her own.
ISBN 0-316-91034-1
[1. Chickens—Fiction. 2. Behavior—Fiction. 3. Friendship—Fiction.] I. Title: Elinor and Violet. II. Title.
PZ7.M9547 Eo 2003
[E]—dc21 2001050196

10 9 8 7 6 5 4 3 2 1

TWP

Printed in Singapore

The paintings for this book were done in gouache on watercolor paper.
The text was set in Bernhard Gothic, and the display type is Providence.

Violet was back, and Elinor's mother was not happy.

Elinor was.

"I don't think Violet is a very good influence on you. You two girls got into a lot of mischief during Violet's visit to her grandmother's last summer," said her mother.

"Not her again," moaned Elinor's sisters.

"Hooray! We're together again!" sang Elinor and Violet.
"Violet is fun," declared Elinor. "She has many good ideas."

"You know," said Elinor's mother, "you don't have to do everything Violet says. If you know it's not right, just tell her it's not a good idea."

But it was hard to say no to Violet. Besides, Elinor was not sure she wanted to. So they reset Elinor's sisters' alarm clock to go off at three A.M. They dyed their clothes purple with Easter egg dye for "Purple Day." They played dress-up with Elinor's sisters' clothes and decorated them with special indelible markers.

Elinor and Violet scooted through the neighbor's garden on

their scooters, snapping off flower heads for flower soup.

The girls collected change from under the cushions in the house. They bought large slingshots and used them.

Violet had learned many new bad words. She shared them with Elinor.

She taught Elinor how to burp loudly whenever she wanted to. It was very useful.

They ate the cookies Elinor's mother was saving for her book club, and they frosted cupcakes with shaving cream.

Elinor sat in the time-out corner once again.

One Saturday morning, Violet said, "We are going to have a grand adventure today. I have an idea. A very good idea. A very, very good idea."

The girls ran down the street. "Hurry up," said Violet, "we have to catch a bus."

"Where are we going?" asked Elinor.

"That," said Violet, "is a surprise."

Elinor felt nervous. But Violet began singing "The Ants Go Marching One by One" in her best opera voice. Elinor joined in loudly.

After a long bus ride, they came to their stop. Elinor could not believe her eyes. They were at the beach!

"Come on," said Violet, "we're going swimming!"

Elinor felt sick.

"We don't have bathing suits," she mumbled.

"So what," said Violet. "We'll swim in our clothes and pretend to be dolphins!"

"This," said Elinor in a shaky voice, "is not a good idea."

Violet narrowed her eyes at Elinor.

"No," said Elinor in a tiny voice, "not this time. We need to have a grown-up with us to swim."

Violet glowered.
Just then another girl bounded up to them.
"Hi, I'm Lulu!"
"Hi," said Violet. "Are you here swimming by yourself?"
"Sure am!"

"See," said Violet to Elinor.
Elinor just looked at the sand.
"Come on," said Lulu. "Last one in is a rotten egg!"
"Don't be a chicken," said Violet.
Elinor just shook her head.

Elinor watched Violet and her new friend cavort in the waves. She felt sad.

After a while, she decided to have a good time on her own. She performed a lovely beach ballet for her fellow sunbathers.

She collected crabs and carefully put them on people's beach towels. But it wasn't much fun without Violet.

"Help!" screamed Violet.
"Help!" screamed Lulu.

They ran onto the beach, yelling, "We've been attacked by a sea monster!"

Elinor rushed to the two girls.

"It's a sea snake!" sobbed Lulu.

"It's just seaweed." Elinor sighed as she untangled the green slippery mass from the girls' legs.

A large chicken came over and scooped up Lulu.

"Are you okay, sweetie?"

"Yes, Mama." Lulu sniffed, not looking at Elinor and Violet.

"Time to go home, anyway," said Lulu's mother as she walked off carrying Lulu.

"Mama?" said Elinor and Violet at the same time.

"So much for the brave girl swimming alone," said Violet. "She wasn't that much fun, anyway. Not like you, Elinor. I'm sorry."

"It's okay," said Elinor. "Things weren't the same without you, either."

Smiling, the girls selected the friskiest crab and put him in an empty yogurt container with a bit of water and brought him home.

On the bus ride back, Violet made up a song about underwear, which they sang in rounds.

They finally arrived at Elinor's house looking hot and bedraggled. Elinor's mother gasped and asked, "Where have you been?"

"We went to the beach," said Elinor. "But don't worry, I didn't swim. I told Violet it wasn't a good idea."

"You did, did you?" said Elinor's mother.

"Yes," said Elinor, "and I'm sorry I didn't tell you where we were going."

"Me, too," said Violet softly.

"And look, here is our new pet crab, Hermie!" Elinor said. "And he has to live at our house, because Violet's grandmother doesn't allow pets."

"Oh, joy," said Elinor's mother.

After Violet went home to change, Elinor's mother hugged her. "You did the right thing, but it was wrong of you to leave without telling me."

"I know," said Elinor.

"It's going to be a long summer." Elinor's mother sighed.
"Hooray!" the girls shouted.

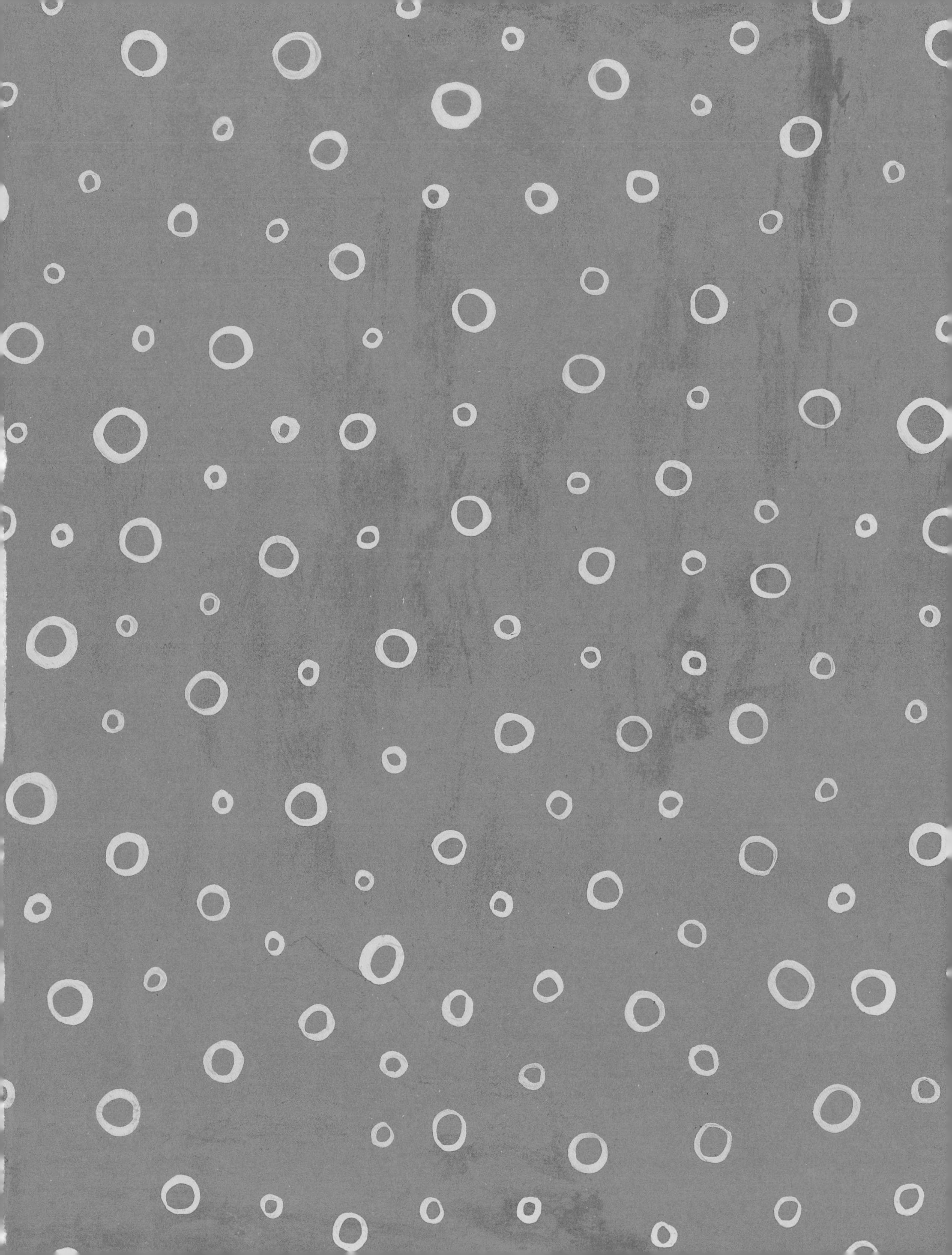

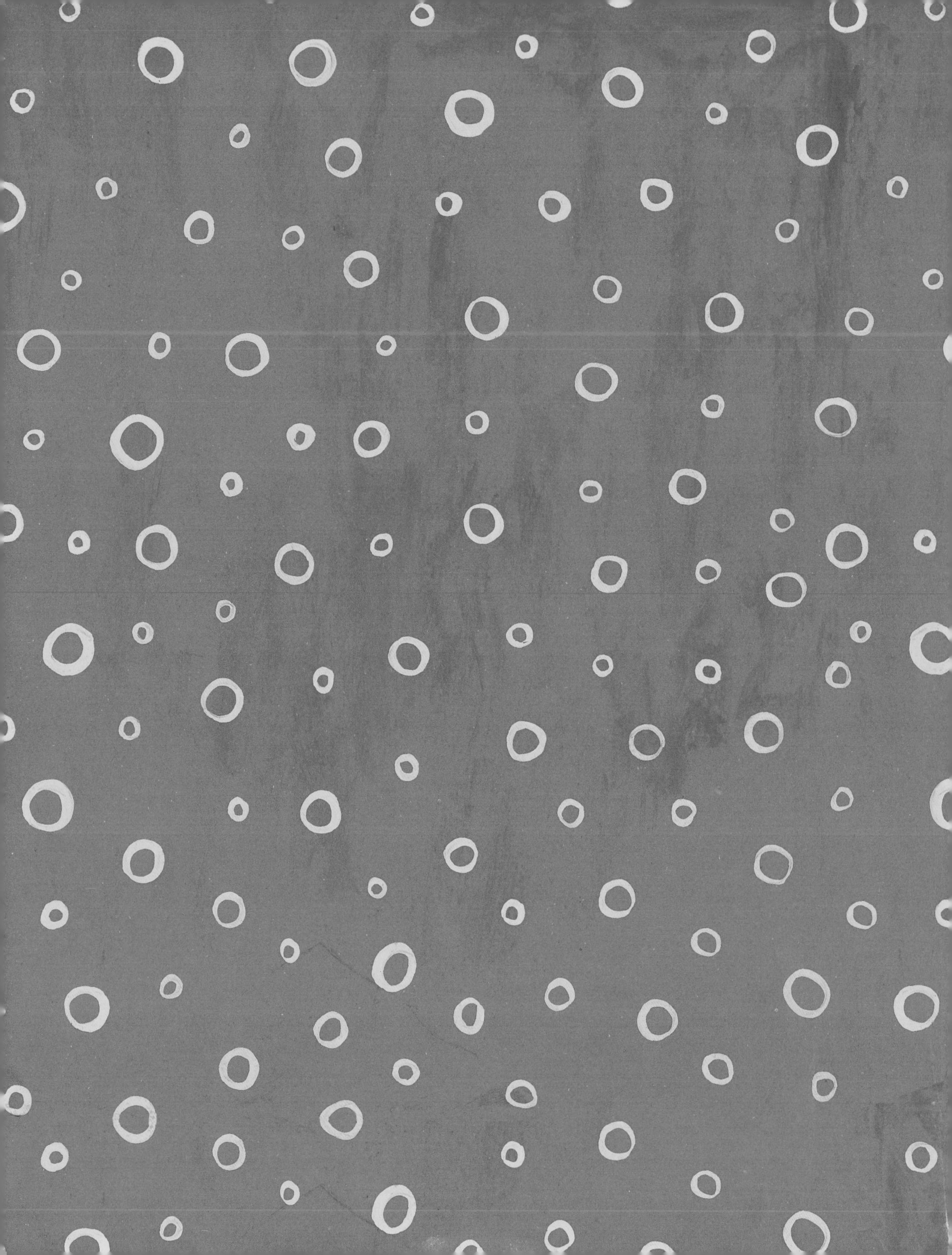